Published simultaneously in 2005 in Great Britain and Canada by
TRADEWIND BOOKS LIMITED **www.tradewindbooks.com**

Distribution and representation in the UK by TURNAROUND www.turnaround-uk.com

Text copyright © 2005 by Sheree Fitch · Illustrations copyright © 2005 by Yayo

Book design by Elisa Gutiérrez

LIBRARY AND ARCHIVES CANADA CATALOGUING IN PUBLICATION

Fitch, Sheree

If I had a million onions / by Sheree Fitch ; illustrated by Yayo.

Poems.

ISBN 1-896580-56-4 (bound).--ISBN 1-896580-78-5 (pbk.)

1. Children's poetry, Canadian (English) I. Yayo II. Title.

PS8561.I86I36 2005   jC811'.54   C2005-902342-2

Printed and bound in China   10   9   8   7   6   5   4   3   2   1

The publisher wishes to thank the Canada Council for the Arts and
the British Columbia Arts Council for their financial support.

Canada Council   Conseil des Arts
for the Arts   du Canada

BRITISH
COLUMBIA
ARTS COUNCIL

Sheree Fitch

illustrations by

Yayo

In memory of Sheldon Oberman—SF

To a greenky-pinky witch's onion breath!—Y

Contents

If I Had a Million Onions

If I had a million onions
I know what I would make
A million onion
Mixed-with-chocolate
Apple honey cake.
I would take some to my teacher
I would feed it to my dad
The best onion
Mixed-with-chocolate
Apple honey cake
They ever had!

If I had a million onions
I suppose I'd cry a sea
Wouldn't it be nifty
If they named it after me?
I'd drift around the world and back
With onion-skins for sails
Past codfish, dolphins, octopi
Beluga baby whales.

If I had a million onions
Then ate them one by one
I'd have a million-onion breath
Wouldn't that be fun?
I could breathe on all the bullies
Save everyone and me
I'd be in all the papers
Have my picture on TV.

If I had a million onions
I know what I would do
I'd make a million onion
Super-duper goopy stew
I would feed it to whoever
Didn't have enough to eat
I would feed it to the raggedies
Who sleep on city streets.

If I had a million onions
I think I'd give them names
Rumpelstiltskin, Jebediah
Jambalaya, Henry James.

If I had a million onions
I would count them every day
I would love them
I would kiss them
I would take them out to play.

I would juggle some
Then huggle some
And give the rest away.

Close Call

A monster came a-knocking
He was hungry as a horse
"Could I join you all for supper?"
We replied, "Uh, yes, of course."

We fed him green tomatoes
Zucchini and roast duck
But for dessert we had to call
A two-ton monster truck

He gobbled up the ice cream
He loved the apple pie
He looked a little sleepy then
Hello! I wonder why!

He curled up on the sofa
Watched gorillas on TV
He had a drink of soda
Then he blinked across at me.

"You look extremely tender.
I think you'd be a treat.
But it seems I've lost my appetite,"
He said and hit the street.

The Saskatchewan Sasquatch

With flannel pink pajamas on
A sasquatch from Saskatchewan
Danced the tango on our lawn
Until at last he yawned and yawned
Then fell asleep when it was dawn
When I woke up?
That sasq was gone!

Argentinosaurus

Argentinosaurus
Is a tenor in the chorus
In an opera that is playing on a stage inside his head.
He's the biggest dinosaurus
He's humongous!
He's enormous!
And his voice is such a roarus he could scare awake the
                                            dead!

Figaro! Figaroo!
I am not a kangaroo!
Figaree! Figurah!
Sol la ti do re mi fa!

Argentinosaurus
Shakes the cities and the forests
Every time he takes a step and sings a score
He is bowing to the tourists who bring flowers from the
                                          florists.
And his dinosaurus chorus is so glorious! Encore!
Figaro! Figaree!
Would you take a look at me!
Figaro! Figara!
Prehistoric opera!

Beggs & Acon

Would you like some beggs and acon?
Would you like a twice of sloast?
Perhaps a cowl of bereal?
What kind you mant the wost?
Do you think my twongue is tisted?
Do you think my thips are lick?
I'll say this all again but
I'll say it queally rick!

If Only I Could Find the Words

It's so marmalade to know you!
I'm so grapefruit to you too!
Many happy gradulations!
You have my symphony, you do.
I think I need a vaccination.
I've heard Hawaii is divine.
Yours truly and for always,
     Love,
          Your secret Turpentine

One Blizzardous Nightstorm

On a blizzardous nightstorm gallotting through slain,
A traveller bravalliant who within't a name
Stampoared through the worests and mounthills and
strooks.

Beceason? His overdue library books!
He frestled a dragster with razordous teeth,
Escaped from the jawtches of blounding to death.
He pinugged his nostrils and volted away,
Arrentered the villtown to people's hallay!

At the string of the clock,
He dropped books in the slot.
Then he burtsied and hurstled away.
All joypy with winumph,
He scrollered.
He laggled.
"Once more I did not have to pay!

"Imagine a plantry where books can be free
Except if you're lardy and must pay a fee.
Like frestling with dragsters, gallotting through slain.
I prow I nevont be forgazy again!

This incredulous strable
Is treal. For of course,
I'm that bravalliant splendificant horse
Who rescaved one reader that blizzardous night,
Who witnessed the blound and partook in the fight.

So if you have probles with overdue fees,
Come learching for me and if you say please,
I'll trollop as swast as I ever have spaced
To save you your digide and not be disgraced.
Just scroller for me.

Rememize my name.
I'm Royal Centurion Oliver James."

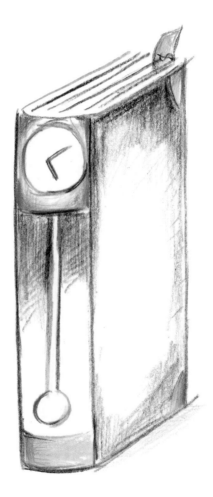

Who Said What When?

Who said one and one are two?
Who said red was red not blue?
Who said sneaker?
Who said shoe?
Who said who?
And me and you?
Who first named the names of words?
Who said fish?
And who said birds?
Imagine saying frying pan.

That's a woman.
That's a man.
Or armadillow.
Pussywillow.
This is soft so call it pillow.
And why are barns all painted red?
And what will happen when I'm dead?
Who said now it's time for bed?
Who put time inside our heads?
Why do children have to grow?
And grown-ups say
"Some day, you'll know."

Sometimes

Sometimes I'm selfish.
Sometimes I'm not.
Sometimes I'd give away
All that I've got.

Sometimes I'm kind.
Sometimes I'm cruel.
Sometimes I'm clever.
Sometimes a fool.

Sometimes I know.
Sometimes I don't.
Sometimes I answer.
Sometimes I won't.

Sometimes I try.
Sometimes I'm lazy.
Sometimes I'm sometimes
A little bit crazy.

Sometimes I'm quiet.
Sometimes I'm loud.
Sometimes I'm guilty.
Sometimes I'm proud.

Sometimes I'm frightened.
Sometimes courageous.
Sometimes I'm healthy.
Sometimes contagious.

Sometimes I'm dirty.
Sometimes I'm clean.
Sometimes I'm living
Somewhere in between.

These are my sometimes.
But most times? I'm Me!
All the time wondering
Who will I be?

A Moving Concrete Poem
Found on a Sidewalk

Amillipedewithhismillionsoffeetisslimingitswayalongourstreetcausingacommotionamiracleofmotionalivingpoemrighttthereifyoulookcloselyandlistenveryveryveryveryverycarefullyandthenifyouareoneofthebraveonestopickitupbeverysogentlethenletthemusicofoneenymillipedeflowrightthroughyoupassitontoafriendandthispoemofthemillipedewillneverneverneverevereverevereverend......

Autumn

In the fall
leaves
   f
      a
        l
          l

Trees are naked and bare
Those trees must freeze
Without their leaves
I'm gonna get them
long
long
long
long
john
underwear!

Bumper Cars

I hop in a new car
A blue car
A new car
But...

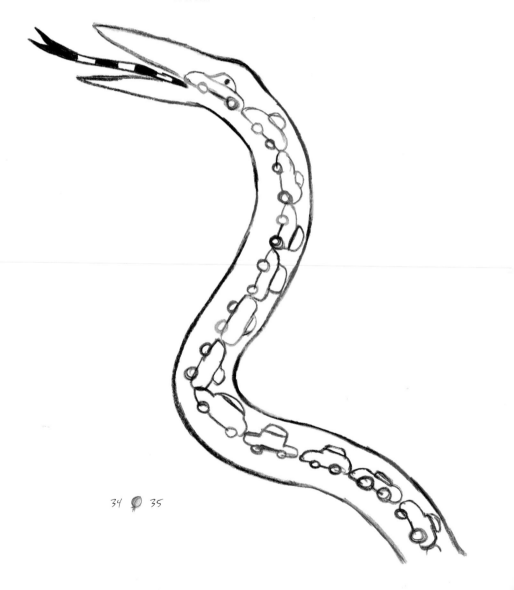

A rubber-bumpered bumper car
Doesn't get very far.
Until BUMP!
Until BAM!
Until THUMPETY-RAM!

Bumper you over there
With the long black hair.
Bumper you in the hat.
Take this!
Take that!

Bumper you in the red.
Bumper me.
I'm ahead.
Bumper you in the green.
Bumper bump
In between.
Bumper you in the black.
Bumper me
Right back.

Bumper-BUMP!
Bumper-BAM!
It's a traffic JAM!
I'm a bumper-car bumper
Bumping BUMPER cars.............BAMMMMMM!

Grampy's Borborygmus

Grampy's borborygmus
Sounds like thunder in the skies.
We all run off for cover,
Plug our noses, close our eyes.

Grampy's borborygmus
Is an earthquake in disguise.
He says:
"Guess I got the gurgulation.
Please excuse me."
Then he sighs.

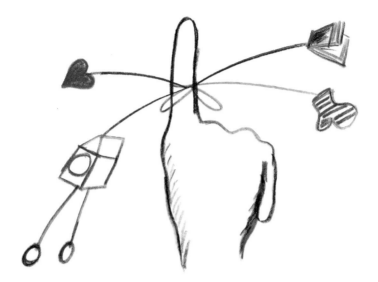

Lost Cause Cousin

Cousin Gloria's notorious
For leaving things behind.
She usually loses mittens
So she wears
One-of-a-kind.
Last year she lost her wallet
And (sigh) her valentine.
Once she lost her temper
It was difficult to find.
She also lost her cuckoo clock.
She's lost a lot of time.
But Gloria's so glorious
She'll make you lose your mind!

Aunt Emma and Uncle Nate

Aunt Emma teaches yoga.
She only drinks chai tea.
Uncle Nate, he meditates
And practises Tai Chi.
My parents send me over
When they've had too much of me.
I love my aunt and uncle
But I wish they'd get TV.

Mr. Little the Whittler

Mr. Little whittled.
He whistled as he whittled.
His wood was pretty brittle
But he whittled anyway.

Mr. Little made a fiddle
That he whittled out of wood.
The fiddle's pretty little
But Little's fiddles
Fiddle good.

Absolutely Gastronomical

Alligator is our waiter.
First customer he had
He ate her!
He said he loved her
Did not hate her
But that was then
Now this is later.

He said he'd never
Eat another.
Crossed his heart
And promised
Mother.
Declared: "From now
And here on in
I'll be a
Vegetarian."

Vanessa Vanastra

Vanessa Vanastra's
A walking disastah.
She fell in a bowlful
Of noodles and pasta.

Now oodles of noodles
Slipdrip from her nose.
Strings of linguini
Hang down to her toes.

She's up to her elbows
In cheese macaroni.
She sneezes lasagna
And meat rigatoni.

Vanessa Vanastra the walking disastah!
If you see her comin'
You betta run fastah.

The Children's News Network

Each night I turn on CNN—
It's the news inside my head,
The only news I ever watch
Before I go to bed.

I'm the producer and the editor.
I do the camera and the sound.
I'm an announcer who enunciates.
I keep the volume down.

Sometimes my name is Zaula Pann.
Sometimes I'm Baren Round.
My teeth are extra pearly white.
I rarely crack a frown.

But my looks are not essential.
For my stories are the best.
I'm contented with my content.
I choose each and every guest.

Sometimes I run the story
Of my sister on the day
They brought her home and told me
She was here to stay.

Sometimes I run the story
Of a boy I used to know
Who used to be a bully
Until the day I told him, "Whoah!"
My news has no commercials.
My news is always breaking.
My news has lots of singing.
And no one's heart is aching.

I have foreign correspondents
Reporting: "Food for everyone!
The world today is filled with peace.
There's no such thing as guns."

This is my good night channel.
Don't need that other stuff.
Least not this late
I'm forty-eight
I'm still not old enough.

Do Your Best Under the Circumstances

There is no land of perfect, child.
There is no sea of ease.
There is no candy apple trail.
There's broccoli and peas.

There is no suit of armour, child.
There's arrows and there's pain.
But when your heart is broken, child
Stay strong and love again.

There is no perfect person, child.
Not presidents or queens.
There's only all us trying, child
To be *human* human beings.

The Most Excellent Advice

Sing a song of cinnamon
A pocketful of spice.
Roll in ravioli.
That's my excellent advice.

Sing a song of joyfulness.
Sing a song of sorrow.
Sing a song of whatyouwish.
Sing a song tomorrow.

Sing a song of doodledang.
Dance an hour away.
My excellent advice is this:
Read a poem a day.

Thinking Happy Thoughts

I love the holes in doughnuts–
You can stick your fingers through.
I love to splash in puddles
Squishing mud-delicious goo.
When I'm itchy I love scratching.
I love picking at my scabs.
Lots of chocolate makes me smile.
So does my Chocolate Lab.

I love to turn chairs upside down–
My tents are excellent!
Banging pots and pans is fun
Until the spoon is bent.

I love rocks in all my pockets.
New sneakers when they squeak.
I love when no one's talking
And I get a chance to speak.

I like cracking ice in puddles.
Spider web designs!
I love a birthday party
When the presents are all mine.

I love blowing big pink bubbles.
I love to crinkle cans.
What makes me happiest of all
Is holding Grampy's hand.

Let Us Play

Let me huddle in the muddle of a slush-delicious mess!
Grass stain green on my knees and bestest dress.
Let me jump in the jungle of the trees in my yard.
I can chirp like the birds if I listen extra hard.

Let me run in the sun on an August afternoon.
Skip in the rain to a raindrop dripping tune.
Let me hop like a rabbit as it scurries on its way.
Let me see, let me touch, let me find, let me play!

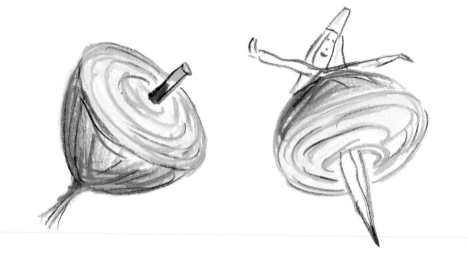

Let me leap like a leopard over shadows that I see!
Run like an antelope where antelopes run free.
Let me giggle in the gaggle of a tag-playing gang.
Let me out, let me in, let me shout, let me bang!
Give me rules to be fair, give me lessons how to share.
But let me wriggle as I figgle all about what is there.
Let me clamber over boulders! Climb the highest hills I find.
Let me do it now and then on my very own time!
In the stormiest of weather
Let us play all together.
Because everyone's
On everybody's team.
In the running and the whying
In the funning and sky-flying
In the hopping and the trying
In the hoping and high-five-ing

Let us play.
Let us play.
Let us dream!

Arctic Lullabye

Arctic high
Arctic low
Arctic beauty
Arctic snow
Arctic char
Ookpik
Bear
Arctic drums
Will lead
Us there.

Arctic caribou
Running wild
Arctic friend
Arctic child
Arctic dreams
Dancing sky
Arctic low
Arctic high.

A Prayer

May no cats get in your sandbox
May your frisbees always spin
May your fridge be filled with oranges
May you love the life you're in.
May your teddy bear be fuzzy
May your rainy days be wet
May your teacher tell you stories
That you never will forget.
May your fingernails get dirty
May your underwear be clean
May your monsters all be friendly
May your grass be mostly green.

May your world spin topsy-turvy
May you love from inside out
May your parents hug you always
May they hardly ever shout.
May your enemies eat sugar
May you play the Superdome
May your friends be slightly crazy
May you always have a home.
May your popsicles stay frozen
May your dreams be true and deep
May you close your eyes and snuggle
May you have a good night's sleep.